CHICK & CHICKIE

PLAY ALL DAY!

Claude Ponti

CHICK & CHICKIE
PLAY ALL DAY!

AAAH!

A TOON BOOK BY

Claude Ponti

TOON BOOKS IS AN IMPRINT OF CANDLE[...]

Visit us at www.abdopublishing.com

Reinforced library bound editions published in 2014 by Spotlight, a division of the ABDO Group, PO Box 398166, Minneapolis, MN 55439. Spotlight produces high-quality reinforced library bound editions for schools and libraries.

Reprinted by agreement with Raw Junior, LLC. All rights reserved.

Printed in the United States of America, North Mankato, Minnesota.

042013
092013

♻ This book contains at least 10% recycled material.

For Adèle

Editorial Director: Françoise Mouly. Book Design: Jonathan Bennett & Françoise Mouly.
Claude Ponti's artwork was done in ink and watercolors.

Library of Congress Cataloging-in-Publication Data
This book was previously cataloged with the following information:

Ponti, Claude, 1948-
Chick & Chickie play all day! / by Claude Ponti.
  p. cm. -- (TOON Books) Based on two of the author's books, previously published in French: Tromboline et Foulbazar : les masques, and Tromboline et Foulbazar : le A.
Summary: Two young chicks have fun making masks and playing with the letter A.
[1. Graphic novels. 2. Chickens--Fiction. 3. Play--Fiction.] I. Title. II. Chick and Chickie Play All Day!
PZ7.7.P66Ch 2012
741.5'944--dc23

                                    2011026764

ISBN 978-1-61479-150-8 (reinforced library bound edition)

What do **you** want
to do?

16

17

19

When we *tickle* the A...

20

THE END

ABOUT THE AUTHOR

CLAUDE PONTI is a prolific author, painter and illustrator, beloved the world over for his humorous explorations of the nonsense world of dreams. The artist created his first picture book, *Adèle's Album,* to amuse his young daughter; he has since authored more than sixty children's books. On a personal note, Claude says: "I'm left-handed; I prefer cats to dogs (they don't lick people); and I'm not a vegetarian because I can't stand the cry of the lettuce or the carrot wrenched from the earth." He also fondly remembers climbing trees as a young boy, looking for the best spot to sit and read a book. He currently divides his time between the French countryside (where there are many birds, such as pheasants) and Paris (where there are pigeons).

HOW TO READ COMICS WITH KIDS

Kids love comics! They are naturally drawn to the details in the pictures, which make them want to read the words. Comics beg for repeated readings and let both emerging and reluctant readers enjoy complex stories with a rich vocabulary. But since comics have their own grammar, here are a few tips for reading them with kids:

GUIDE YOUNG READERS: Use your finger to show your place in the text, but keep it at the bottom of the speaking character so it doesn't hide the very important facial expressions.

HAM IT UP! Think of the comic book story as a play and don't hesitate to read with expression and intonation. Assign parts or get kids to supply the sound effects, a great way to reinforce phonics skills.

LET THEM GUESS. Comics provide lots of context for the words, so emerging readers can make informed guesses. Like jigsaw puzzles, comics ask readers to make connections, so check a young audience's understanding by asking "What's this character thinking?" (but don't be surprised if a kid finds some of the comics' subtle details faster than you).

TALK ABOUT THE PICTURES. Point out how the artist paces the story with pauses (silent panels) or speeded-up action (a burst of short panels). Discuss how the size and shape of the panels carry meaning.

ABOVE ALL, ENJOY! There is of course never one right way to read, so go for the shared pleasure. Once children make the story happen in their imagination, they have discovered the thrill of reading, and you won't be able to stop them. At that point, just go get them more books, and more comics.

www.TOON-BOOKS.com

SEE OUR FREE ONLINE CARTOON MAKERS, LESSON PLANS, AND MUCH MORE

TOON into Reading

LEVEL 1

FIRST COMICS FOR BRAND-NEW READERS

GRADES K–1 • LEXILE BR–100
GUIDED READING A–G • READING RECOVERY 7–10

- 200–300 easy sight words
- short sentences
- often one character
- single time frame or theme
- 1–2 panels per page

LEVEL 2

EASY-TO-READ COMICS FOR EMERGING READERS

GRADES 1–2 • LEXILE BR–170
GUIDED READING G–J • READING RECOVERY 11–17

- 300–600 words
- short sentences and repetition
- story arc with few characters in a small world
- 1–4 panels per page

LEVEL 3

CHAPTER-BOOK COMICS FOR ADVANCED BEGINNERS

GRADES 2–3 • LEXILE 150–300
GUIDED READING J–N • READING RECOVERY 17–19

- 800+ words in long sentences
- broad world as well as shifts in time and place
- long story divided in chapters
- reader needs to make connections and speculate